Meet ME Where I'm At

Cindy Best and Joyce Shor Johnson

Meet Me Where I'm At

All marketing and publishing rights guaranteed to and reserved by:

FUTURE HORIZONS INC.

721 W. Abram St. Arlington, TX 76013

Toll-free: 800·489·0727 | Fax: 817·277·2270

www.FHautism.com | info@FHautism.com

ISBN: 9781941765395

A Note From Cindy

Meet Me Where I'm At was inspired by the many gifted and spirited children I work with at A.R.T.S. and the two incredible sons I've raised. The title comes from the perspective of a child with special needs and serves as a reminder to meet him where he is at—not where you would like him to be—because for him, that place can change from moment to moment.

This book was originally created as a visual tool for my son's "toolbox." When my son was young, I knew he needed a guidebook in order for his teachers to understand him. As he grew older, I wanted him to have a way to inform each teacher, coach, or adult he encountered along his journey that this is how he is wired. This book enabled him to advocate for himself.

paste
photo here

The layout of this book allows you to decide what pages help you to understand yourself. Now, you can design and create a book about you to share with family members, teachers, coaches, and friends.

This book belongs to _____

Just because I'm not using my words to tell you what I feel . . . doesn't mean I'm not trying to tell you something very important.

Meet me where I'm at.

Give me extra time to try to find my words. Look at my face and my body. What are they showing? Frustration? Anger? Anxiety? Excitement?

Provide me with a way to tell you . . .

Sign language, a picture board, art supplies, or a computer.

What works best for me is

_____!

Just because I'm not looking at you. . .

doesn't mean I'm not listening.

Meet me
where I'm at.

If I look you in the eye when you are talking to me,
it overloads my brain with too much information.

My ears work best
when my eyes don't have to work, too.

Just because I'm behaving badly . . . doesn't mean I'm a bad kid

Meet me where I'm at.

I am feeling like an animal backed into a corner. I am overwhelmed, scared, frustrated, anxious, and maybe even angry.

I want you to . . .

Understand that when I want to hit you, it is to tell you to stop confronting me. Sometimes I need to run away and hide to work through how I feel.

When I hit or run away and hide, usually I am feeling . . .

_____

_____

_____

Just because I'm not quietly sitting in my seat . . . doesn't mean I'm not doing my schoolwork.

Meet me where I'm at.

I need to move to understand what you are teaching me. I need to think through a question out loud before I can give you an answer.

To learn best, sometimes I need to . . .

_____

_____

_____

_____

_____

Just because I'm listening to music . . . doesn't mean I'm not getting my homework done.

Meet me where I'm at.

My brain is a busy place with lots of thoughts constantly flying through it. Music helps to quiet the noise in my head and helps me focus on my work.

My favorite music is

_____

_____

Just because It's hard for me to write with a pencil and paper. . . doesn't mean I don't have a lot to say.

Meet me where I'm at.

I have an incredible imagination with lots of stories in my head. On the computer I am able to type out my ideas almost as fast as they come into my head. Paper and pencil take me so long, I often forget the idea by the time I start to write it out.

My ideas:

1. _____

2. _____

3. _____

4. _____

5. _____

Just because I interrupt you . . . doesn't mean I'm not interested in what you have to say.

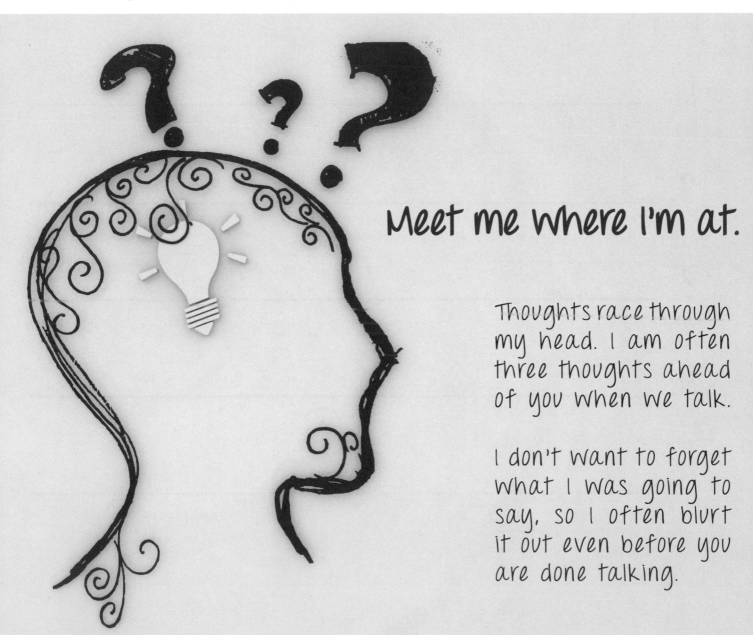

Meet me where I'm at.

Thoughts race through my head. I am often three thoughts ahead of you when we talk.

I don't want to forget what I was going to say, so I often blurt it out even before you are done talking.

Just because I'm not doing what you've asked me to do . . . doesn't mean I don't want to do it.

Meet me where I'm at.

I don't handle change well. Moving from one activity to another or doing something different from my usual routine is very hard for me. It takes me a long time to shift to something new. Often, by the time I finally adjust and settle in, it's time to change activities again. I get stuck and overwhelmed all over again. Give me extra time. Give me verbal cues and a visual calendar and clock to help me prepare for what is coming next.

I can move from one activity to the next when I . . .

_____

_____

_____

_____

I am a very concrete, black-and-white thinker.

If you tell me "we'll cross that bridge when we get there," I will ask you "what bridge?"

Just because I'm speaking loudly . . . doesn't mean I am trying to disrupt class.

Meet me where I'm at.

I have a very difficult time controlling the volume of my voice, especially when I am upset or excited. I am very sensitive and my emotions tend to be intense, often making my reaction to a situation extreme.

To quiet myself down, I . . .

_____

_____

_____

_____

Just because I may be loud . . . doesn't mean I like loud noises. Birthday parties, lunchrooms, and other places with lots of people and noise overwhelm me.

Meet me where I'm at.

Allow me to leave and eat my lunch in a quiet place or play alone in another room while the party is going on.

When the world
around me feels loud,
I like to . . .

_____

_____

_____

_____

Just because I'm off on my own . . . doesn't mean I don't want to play on the team.

Meet me where I'm at.

Practice is held in an open space with lots of people, sights, and sounds. On top of that, I have a coach who is giving me lots of instructions. I am totally overwhelmed. I cannot focus on coach's directions, but want to play. I go off in the corner and play alone. Coach thinks I am being disrespectful and not listening.

Game time is different for me. It is fast paced. I can move and act impulsively which is how I work best.

My favorite activity is _____.

Just because I'm not always good with people . . . doesn't mean I'm not compassionate.

Meet me where I'm at.

I often feel misunderstood by people. Watch me with animals. I have a natural ability to communicate with them. They don't use their words either. But I know what they need or want. I know how to love and care for them without them telling me with words.

My favorite animal is _____.

This is who I am and how I am wired. I have many incredible, special gifts. I am creative, imaginative, and passionate.

I may not be the easiest kid to be friends with or parent, but I am so worth the effort.

Meet me . . . outside the norm.
That is where you will find me.

I am the turbulent, indigo crayon that does not fit into the standard crayon box. If you try to squeeze me into the box, I will not bend but break.

Who wants to be stuck in a standard box of crayons, anyway? It's crowded in there.

Besides, you won't find the likes of Thomas Edison, Bill Gates, or the person I am going to grow up to be in a standard box of crayons!

Believe in me and what I am made of.

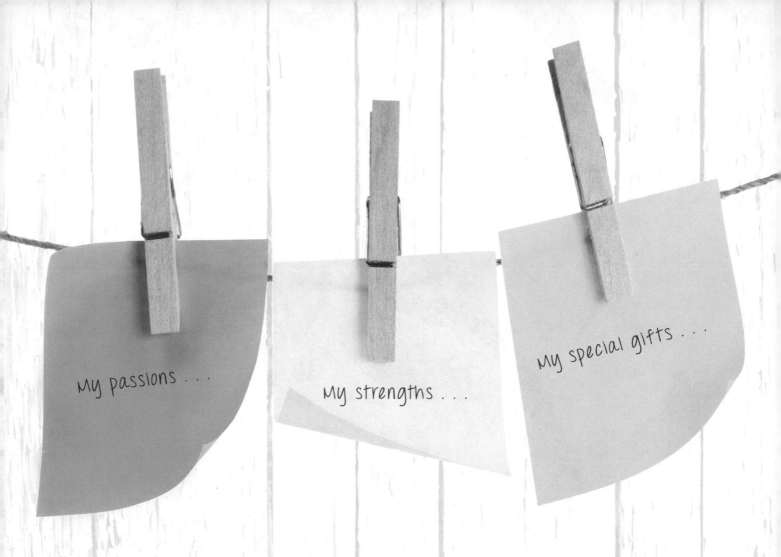

My passions . . .

My strengths . . .

My special gifts . . .

Help me find my passions, strengths, and special gifts.

Help me find my fire
and feel my wings.

Meet me where I'm at!

Cindy Best M.S., P.T., has been a pediatric physical therapist and an artist for over 20 years. She is the creator of **A.R.T.S.: Adaptive Art, Respite, and Therapeutic Play Services**. A.R.T.S. is a non-profit dedicated to helping children with special needs find their passions, strengths, and special gifts. Cindy was diagnosed with ADHD as an adult. She works with children of all abilities, but primarily children on the autism spectrum. She is the loving mom to two amazing sons, one with ADHD and the other with mild autism. She is grateful for the pieces of ADHD and autism in herself and her children, for it is these pieces that help to make each of them the amazing, spirited, and passionate people they are. She lives in a little log cabin at the base of Mt. Kearsarge in New Hampshire. A.R.T.S. weekly classes and summer camp are nestled into the barn next door.

A.R.T.S.

Joyce Shor Johnson, B.S., M.F.A., is a published author and former teacher who taught learning skills to high school students at a private school in New Hampshire. Joyce was drawn to the **A.R.T.S.: Adaptive Art, Respite, and Therapeutic Play Services** book project because she believes it is a valuable tool that will empower children with autism and special needs by helping families, teachers, friends, and the community at large to understand and appreciate these amazing kids. Joyce is the mom to two incredible teens who have alternative learning styles.

You can learn more about Joyce at www.joyceshorjohnson.com

A Percentage of Proceeds From This Book

are donated to A.R.T.S. to provide children scholarships to weekly A.R.T.S. classes and Summer Adaptive Art Camp. Proceeds will also continue the publication and promotion of MEET ME WHERE I'M AT as a resource for children, families, educators, coaches, and counselors.

A.R.T.S.

Adaptive art, Respite, & Therapeutic play Services.

* Adaptive art classes for children with special needs.
* Respite opportunities for parents and caregivers.
* Therapeutic play at Summer Adaptive Art Camps and weekly A.R.T.S. classes.

Offering:

♡ WEEKLY CLASSES
♡ SUMMER CAMP

Do you have a suggestion for a page that might help someone talk about where they are at?

Send your suggestion to us at
https://www.facebook.com/MeetMeWhereImAtbook

Other Children's Books for Kids with Autism and Their Friends